Is Everything Okay?

One-Sentence Conversations for When Love, Attachment, and Emotions Feel Confusing

Johanna Sparrow

A Gentle Note Before We Begin

This book is meant to support reflection, awareness, and emotional understanding.

It is not a substitute for therapy, medical care, or professional mental health treatment. Nothing in these pages is intended to diagnose you, someone you love, or anyone else.

If reading this book brings up strong emotional reactions, distress, or memories that feel overwhelming, please consider reaching out to a qualified mental health professional or a trusted support person.

This book is not here to tell you who you are.
It's here to help you notice what you're feeling — with compassion.

Use what resonates.
Leave what doesn't.
And take care of yourself as you read.

Table of Contents

Part III: Dismissive / Avoidant Attachment Behaviors

When Distance Feels Safer Than Closeness

When emotions feel overwhelming
When shutting down feels easier than explaining
When space feels like relief
When independence feels protective
When closeness triggers withdrawal

Part IV: Fearful-Avoidant Attachment Behaviors

When You Want Closeness and Fear It at the Same Time

When intensity feels familiar
When you pull away after opening up
When reassurance feels unsafe
When emotions shift quickly
When connection feels both comforting and threatening

Part V: Secure Attachment Responses

What Regulation and Clarity Can Look Like

When you pause instead of react
When you name needs without apologizing
When conflict doesn't mean loss
When boundaries don't remove love
When calm begins to feel safe

Introduction

Hey.

I know this isn't the kind of book you pick up casually.

People usually come here because something just happened—or keeps happening—and they don't know what to do with how it landed. They're trying to stay calm, stay reasonable, stay kind… while something inside them feels unsettled.

So let me ask you the question the way I actually mean it.

Is everything okay?

And you don't have to answer out loud.
You don't have to make it sound better than it is.
You don't even have to know the answer yet.

Just notice what your body does when you hear it.

Most of the time, it's not one big thing that brings someone here.
It's a moment.

Someone goes quiet after an argument.
A message doesn't come back.
Closeness shows up—and suddenly feels like too much.
You feel connected one minute and strangely alone the next.

And then comes the spiral of questions:

Am I overthinking this?
Am I asking for too much?
Why does this affect me so deeply?

If that sounds familiar, I want you to hear this clearly:

There is nothing wrong with you.

What you're experiencing isn't drama.
It's information.

I wrote this book the way I talk to the people I care about
most—when they finally tell me what's been happening
and I can hear the confusion underneath their words.

Each page starts with a real situation.
Not theory. Not abstraction.
The kind of moment people usually brush off or blame
themselves for.

Then I reflect back what's actually happening beneath the
surface—often through the lens of attachment and nervous
system responses. Not to label you. Not to label anyone
else. Just to bring clarity where there's been self-doubt.

And finally, I offer something simple: what helps, and what
usually makes things harder.

No fixing.
No forcing.
Just steadiness.

This isn't a book you read straight through to be "done."
It's a book you come back to when something happens and
you need to ground yourself before reacting.

You'll notice I talk about attachment styles in these
pages—anxious, dismissive, fearful, secure.

I'm not interested in using these as boxes or excuses.
I use them because they explain *patterns*.

Attachment styles are simply the ways we learned to stay
safe in connection. They form early. They make sense once
you understand the environment they came from.

If you've ever:

- felt panicked when someone pulled away
- felt overwhelmed when someone got close
- wanted reassurance and then felt ashamed for
  needing it
- shut down even though you cared

You're not broken.
Your nervous system learned how to protect you.

This book helps you see those responses without turning on
yourself.

One gentle boundary before you continue.

This book is not meant to diagnose your partner, your ex, or anyone else. If a page reminds you of someone, that's information—not ammunition.

The real power here is what happens when *you* understand your responses well enough to pause, regulate, and choose how you want to show up.

Clarity without cruelty.
Insight without self-blame.

If you're here because you feel confused, tired, or quietly overwhelmed, I'm really glad you found your way here.

You don't need answers yet.
You don't need to make decisions today.

We'll take this one moment at a time.

I'm right here with you.

PART I

Opening the Conversation

Page Prompt
So everything looks fine on the outside, but your body feels tight?

Reflection
Your nervous system often registers discomfort before your mind is ready to acknowledge it.

Do / Don't
Do: Pause and notice what your body is signaling.
Don't: Dismiss the feeling just because nothing "big" happened.

Page Prompt
So the conversation ended, but you don't feel settled?

Reflection
Unresolved emotional moments can leave your system on
alert, even without obvious conflict.

Do / Don't
Do: Name the unsettled feeling to yourself.
Don't: Force closure just to feel okay.

Page Prompt
So you keep replaying what you said, wondering if you
said too much?

Reflection
This often comes from past experiences where honesty felt
risky or costly.

Do / Don't
Do: Remind yourself that expressing emotion isn't a
mistake.
Don't: Turn reflection into self-blame.

Page Prompt
So nothing is technically wrong, but you don't feel calm?

Reflection
Emotional safety isn't logical—it's somatic.

Do / Don't
Do: Trust your internal experience.
Don't: Gaslight yourself with "I should be fine."

Page Prompt
So you're waiting to see what happens before letting
yourself relax?

Reflection
When predictability was missing before, your system
learned to stay alert.

Do / Don't
Do: Ground yourself in what's happening right now.
Don't: Borrow fear from the future.

Page Prompt
So you're trying to understand what they meant instead of
how it felt?

Reflection
Over-analyzing meaning can override your emotional
reality.

Do / Don't
Do: Name the feeling before searching for explanations.
Don't: Abandon your experience to preserve connection.

Page Prompt
So you adjusted yourself again to keep things smooth?

Reflection
Over-accommodation often forms when being "easy" once
felt necessary to stay close.

Do / Don't
Do: Acknowledge the effort you're making.
Don't: Shrink yourself to earn stability.

Page Prompt
So part of you feels connected, and part of you feels alone?

Reflection
Mixed signals—internal or external—create emotional
confusion.

Do / Don't
Do: Validate the contradiction.
Don't: Force clarity before you're regulated.

Page Prompt
So you're bracing for something even when things are
going well?

Reflection
Anticipating loss can feel safer than being surprised by it.

Do / Don't
Do: Notice when you're guarding joy.
Don't: Punish yourself for wanting things to last.

Page Prompt
So is everything okay—or are you finally paying attention?

Reflection
Awareness is often the first act of self-trust.

Do / Don't
Do: Let yourself be exactly where you are.
Don't: Rush to resolve what's still unfolding.

PART II

Anxious Attachment Behaviors

Page Prompt
So you're checking your phone even though you already looked a minute ago?

Reflection
This is your nervous system searching for reassurance when connection feels uncertain.

Do / Don't
Do: Take one slow breath before checking again.
Don't: Shame yourself for wanting closeness.

Page Prompt
So their reply instantly calmed you—and their silence
instantly didn't?

Reflection
Anxious attachment often ties emotional regulation to
external responses.

Do / Don't
Do: Notice the shift without judging it.
Don't: Let response time define your worth.

Page Prompt
So you're rereading messages to see if you said something
wrong?

Reflection
When connection has felt fragile before, your mind scans
for mistakes.

Do / Don't
Do: Gently remind yourself that honesty isn't an error.
Don't: Turn self-reflection into self-attack.

Page Prompt
So silence feels louder than anything they actually said?

Reflection
Silence can register as threat when abandonment has been a real possibility.

Do / Don't
Do: Ground yourself in what you know, not what you fear.
Don't: Fill the gap with worst-case stories.

Page Prompt
So you want reassurance but feel embarrassed for needing
it?

Reflection
Needing reassurance doesn't mean you're weak—it means
your system is asking for safety.

Do / Don't
Do: Offer yourself reassurance first.
Don't: Turn a need into a flaw.

Page Prompt
So you feel an urge to fix things right now so the
discomfort stops?

Reflection
Urgency often appears when emotional uncertainty feels
unsafe.

Do / Don't
Do: Slow your body before solving anything.
Don't: Force resolution to escape anxiety.

Page Prompt
So you're taking responsibility for their mood?

Reflection
Anxious attachment can blur emotional boundaries in the
name of connection.

Do / Don't
Do: Ask yourself what actually belongs to you.
Don't: Carry emotions that aren't yours.

Page Prompt
So you're afraid that if you stop reaching out, everything
will fall apart?

Reflection
This fear often forms when connection once felt
conditional.

Do / Don't
Do: Experiment with small pauses and notice what comes
up.
Don't: Abandon yourself to maintain closeness.

Page Prompt
So you feel like you're trying harder than they are?

Reflection
Imbalance can activate abandonment fear and intensify
anxious patterns.

Do / Don't
Do: Observe the effort without self-blame.
Don't: Chase consistency at the cost of self-respect.

Page Prompt
So you feel emotionally exhausted but still can't let go?

Reflection
Anxious attachment can confuse intensity with intimacy.

Do / Don't
Do: Rest your nervous system before deciding anything.
Don't: Interpret exhaustion as failure.

Page Prompt
So you're watching for signs you're losing them?

Reflection
Your mind is trying to protect you by predicting pain.

Do / Don't
Do: Notice when prediction replaces presence.
Don't: Treat anxiety as intuition without grounding.

Page Prompt
So you feel guilty for needing consistency?

Reflection
Consistency isn't asking for too much—it's a basic
attachment need.

Do / Don't
Do: Separate needs from self-judgment.
Don't: Talk yourself out of what steadies you.

Page Prompt
So reassurance helps, but only for a moment?

Reflection
External reassurance can't fully replace internal safety.

Do / Don't
Do: Build safety through grounding and self-attunement.
Don't: Judge yourself for being in the process.

Page Prompt
So you feel deeply—and wonder why others don't?

Reflection
Depth of feeling isn't a weakness—it's sensitivity without regulation.

Do / Don't
Do: Honor your capacity for connection.
Don't: Compare your inner world to someone else's outside.

Page Prompt
So what if your anxiety isn't trying to ruin your
relationship—but protect it?

Reflection
Anxious attachment developed to preserve connection, not
sabotage it.

Do / Don't
Do: Thank your system for trying to help.
Don't: Let protection turn into self-attack.

PART III

Dismissive / Avoidant Attachment Behaviors

Page Prompt
So after the argument, you went quiet instead of talking it through?

Reflection
When emotions feel overwhelming, avoidant coping often chooses distance to regain control.

Do / Don't
Do: Give yourself space without disappearing completely.
Don't: Assume silence will resolve what needs understanding.

Page Prompt
So you told yourself it didn't bother you—even though it did?

Reflection
Minimizing emotions can be a learned way to stay functional and self-contained.

Do / Don't
Do: Acknowledge what you felt privately first.
Don't: Confuse emotional restraint with emotional honesty.

Page Prompt
So closeness felt good—and then suddenly felt like too
much?

Reflection
Intimacy can trigger fear of losing autonomy when
independence once felt safer.

Do / Don't
Do: Notice the shift without judging it.
Don't: Pull away abruptly to regulate.

Page Prompt
So you needed space, but didn't explain why?

Reflection
Avoidant attachment often assumes others won't
understand emotional needs.

Do / Don't
Do: Name your need for space simply, when you can.
Don't: Leave the other person guessing.

Page Prompt
So emotional conversations make you feel trapped?

Reflection
When feelings once felt unsafe, your system learned to
disengage to stay steady.

Do / Don't
Do: Ground your body before exiting the conversation.
Don't: Shut down completely to escape discomfort.

Page Prompt
So you feel more comfortable fixing things than talking
about feelings?

Reflection
Competence can feel safer than vulnerability when
emotions weren't reliably met.

Do / Don't
Do: Notice how you show care through action.
Don't: Avoid emotional presence entirely.

Page Prompt
So you feel calm alone—but tense in emotional closeness?

Reflection
Solitude can feel regulating when connection once felt
unpredictable.

Do / Don't
Do: Honor your need for alone time.
Don't: Use distance to avoid all intimacy.

Page Prompt
So you intellectualize what happened instead of feeling it?

Reflection
Thinking can become a shield when emotions feel too
intense to hold.

Do / Don't
Do: Allow thought and feeling to coexist.
Don't: Use logic to bypass emotion.

Page Prompt
So you're irritated when someone needs reassurance from
you?

Reflection
Needs can feel like pressure when self-reliance was once
necessary for safety.

Do / Don't
Do: Separate the request from the threat you feel.
Don't: Judge yourself for wanting autonomy.

Page Prompt
So you pull back after moments of closeness?

Reflection
After intimacy, avoidant systems often need space to re-regulate.

Do / Don't
Do: Take space with intention.
Don't: Disappear without explanation.

Page Prompt
So conflict makes you want to end the conversation
quickly?

Reflection
When repair wasn't modeled, disengagement became the
safest exit.

Do / Don't
Do: Pause the conversation instead of abandoning it.
Don't: Assume distance is the only solution.

Page Prompt
So being needed feels overwhelming instead of
comforting?

Reflection
Dependence can feel threatening when independence was
once essential.

Do / Don't
Do: Notice what level of closeness feels manageable.
Don't: Turn overwhelm into emotional shutdown.

Page Prompt
So you feel misunderstood when others say you're distant?

Reflection
Avoidant attachment doesn't lack feeling—it protects it.

Do / Don't
Do: Recognize the care you express quietly.
Don't: Accept labels that erase your inner experience.

Page Prompt
So you prefer low expectations because they feel safer?

Reflection
Low expectation can feel like freedom when obligation
once felt heavy.

Do / Don't
Do: Notice how safety feels in your body.
Don't: Confuse emotional neutrality with fulfillment.

Page Prompt
So what if your distance isn't disinterest—but regulation?

Reflection
Avoidant attachment formed to preserve stability, not to
avoid love.

Do / Don't
Do: Offer yourself compassion for how you learned to
cope.
Don't: Let self-protection turn into self-disconnection.

PART IV

Fearful-Avoidant Attachment Behaviors

Page Prompt
So you want closeness badly—and then panic when it actually happens?

Reflection
Fearful-avoidant attachment forms when connection has felt both comforting and unsafe.

Do / Don't
Do: Slow the pace of intimacy.
Don't: Shame yourself for the contradiction.

Page Prompt
So you open up, and then immediately wish you hadn't?

Reflection
Vulnerability can trigger fear when being seen once led to
unpredictability.

Do / Don't
Do: Give yourself time to re-regulate after sharing.
Don't: Retract truth out of fear.

Page Prompt
So you feel deeply attached one moment—and strangely
detached the next?

Reflection
Your nervous system shifts quickly to protect you from
emotional overload.

Do / Don't
Do: Notice the shift before acting on it.
Don't: Assume the feeling means something is wrong.

Page Prompt
So reassurance feels comforting—and then suddenly feels unsafe?

Reflection
Care can activate fear when closeness once came with inconsistency.

Do / Don't
Do: Let reassurance land slowly.
Don't: Force yourself to accept comfort all at once.

Page Prompt
So you crave intensity because calm feels unfamiliar?

Reflection
Intensity can feel like connection when consistency was
missing early on.

Do / Don't
Do: Notice how intensity affects your body.
Don't: Mistake adrenaline for intimacy.

Page Prompt
So you pull away after moments of emotional closeness?

Reflection
After vulnerability, fearful-avoidant systems often need distance to feel safe again.

Do / Don't
Do: Take space with awareness.
Don't: Cut ties abruptly to regain control.

Page Prompt
So you feel responsible for managing everyone's
emotions—including your own?

Reflection
Hyper-vigilance often develops when emotional
environments felt unpredictable.

Do / Don't
Do: Identify where responsibility ends.
Don't: Carry emotional weight that isn't yours.

Page Prompt
So you fear abandonment—but also fear being fully seen?

Reflection
Being known can feel as threatening as being left when
safety was inconsistent.

Do / Don't
Do: Let connection unfold in layers.
Don't: Demand total closeness all at once.

Page Prompt
So your reactions surprise you after the moment passes?

Reflection
Fearful-avoidant responses often make sense only once the
nervous system settles.

Do / Don't
Do: Reflect later with compassion.
Don't: Rewrite your story to punish yourself.

Page Prompt
So you feel too much and then feel nothing at all?

Reflection
This swing is a protective response—not instability.

Do / Don't
Do: Anchor yourself in the present moment.
Don't: Label yourself as broken.

Page Prompt
So you test connection instead of trusting it?

Reflection
Testing is a survival strategy when trust once felt
dangerous.

Do / Don't
Do: Notice the urge without acting on it.
Don't: Create rupture to feel important.

Page Prompt
So closeness feels safer when it stays brief?

Reflection
Short-lived intensity can feel manageable when sustained
connection feels risky.

Do / Don't
Do: Pace emotional closeness intentionally.
Don't: Confuse fleeting connection with depth.

Page Prompt
So you feel ashamed for wanting closeness so much?

Reflection
Shame often forms when emotional needs were
inconsistently met.

Do / Don't
Do: Normalize your longing.
Don't: Turn need into self-criticism.

Page Prompt
So relationships bring out both your best and your worst?

Reflection
Fearful-avoidant attachment amplifies longing and fear at the same time.

Do / Don't
Do: Separate who you are from how you react.
Don't: Let reactions define your worth.

Page Prompt
So what if your push-pull isn't sabotage—but a nervous system asking for safety?

Reflection
Fearful-avoidant attachment formed to survive unpredictability, not to destroy connection.

Do / Don't
Do: Offer yourself patience and time.
Don't: Confuse healing with urgency.

PART V

Secure Attachment Responses

Page Prompt
So you notice the feeling without immediately reacting to it?

Reflection
Secure attachment allows emotions to exist without turning them into action right away.

Do / Don't
Do: Pause and breathe before responding.
Don't: Rush to fix discomfort.

Page Prompt
So you name what you need without apologizing for
needing it?

Reflection
Security doesn't erase needs—it trusts they can be
expressed.

Do / Don't
Do: Speak plainly and calmly.
Don't: Minimize your needs to avoid tension.

Page Prompt
So you stay present even when the conversation feels
uncomfortable?

Reflection
Secure attachment tolerates discomfort in service of
understanding.

Do / Don't
Do: Stay curious instead of defensive.
Don't: Mistake discomfort for danger.

Page Prompt
So you listen without preparing your response?

Reflection
Feeling safe inside yourself makes it easier to hear others
clearly.

Do / Don't
Do: Focus on understanding, not winning.
Don't: Turn conversation into self-protection.

Page Prompt
So you trust consistency instead of scanning for signs it
will disappear?

Reflection
Security rests in stability rather than anticipation of loss.

Do / Don't
Do: Let calm moments be calm.
Don't: Sabotage safety to feel intensity.

Page Prompt
So you tolerate space without assuming abandonment?

Reflection
Space supports individuality when attachment is secure.

Do / Don't
Do: Use space to reconnect with yourself.
Don't: Fill silence with fear-based stories.

Page Prompt
So you repair after conflict instead of retreating or
escalating?

Reflection
Security prioritizes repair over being right.

Do / Don't
Do: Return to the conversation when regulated.
Don't: Let pride block reconnection.

Page Prompt
So you accept reassurance when it's offered?

Reflection
Secure attachment allows care to land without suspicion.

Do / Don't
Do: Let support reach you.
Don't: Push away kindness to maintain control.

Page Prompt
So you hold boundaries without withdrawing love?

Reflection
Boundaries protect connection—they don't threaten it.

Do / Don't
Do: Be clear and kind together.
Don't: Use distance as punishment.

Page Prompt
So you trust that disagreement doesn't equal
disconnection?

Reflection
Secure attachment understands that conflict and connection
can coexist.

Do / Don't
Do: Stay grounded during disagreement.
Don't: Assume the relationship is ending.

Page Prompt
So you allow imperfection without taking it personally?

Reflection
Security separates behavior from worth—yours and theirs.

Do / Don't
Do: Allow room for humanity.
Don't: Internalize every misstep.

Page Prompt
So you choose clarity even when it feels vulnerable?

Reflection
Security values truth over emotional guessing games.

Do / Don't
Do: Ask direct questions.
Don't: Expect mind-reading.

Page Prompt
So you stay connected to yourself while being close to
someone else?

Reflection
Secure attachment balances intimacy with autonomy.

Do / Don't
Do: Keep your inner world active.
Don't: Disappear into the relationship.

Page Prompt
So you trust your ability to handle whatever comes next?

Reflection
Security isn't certainty—it's confidence in your resilience.

Do / Don't
Do: Remember past resilience.
Don't: Depend on control to feel safe.

Page Prompt
So what if security isn't who you are—but what you
practice?

Reflection
Secure attachment grows through repeated regulated
responses.

Do / Don't
Do: Practice one steady response at a time.
Don't: Turn growth into performance.

PART VI

Attachment Pairings

Page Prompt
So you reach for closeness, and they seem to relax when
you stop?

Reflection
Anxious–avoidant pairings often create a loop where one
seeks connection and the other seeks relief.

Do / Don't
Do: Ground yourself before responding to the distance.
Don't: Chase withdrawal hoping it turns into closeness.

Page Prompt
So things feel closest right before someone pulls away?

Reflection
In anxious–avoidant dynamics, intimacy can activate fear
on both sides.

Do / Don't
Do: Notice the timing without personalizing it.
Don't: Assume closeness caused harm.

Page Prompt
So you're explaining your needs while they're explaining
their independence?

Reflection
Both partners are protecting something—just in opposite
directions.

Do / Don't
Do: Listen for the fear underneath the words.
Don't: Compete over whose needs matter more.

Page Prompt
So conversations feel intense, emotional, and unresolved?

Reflection
When two dysregulated nervous systems meet, clarity often
gets lost.

Do / Don't
Do: Pause the conversation earlier than usual.
Don't: Wait until exhaustion forces an ending.

Page Prompt
So you feel bonded through conflict more than calm?

Reflection
For some pairings, intensity becomes the main access point
to connection.

Do / Don't
Do: Build closeness during neutral moments.
Don't: Use conflict to feel close.

Page Prompt
So one of you feels like "too much" and the other "not enough"?

Reflection
This polarity is common in anxious–dismissive relationships and feeds misunderstanding.

Do / Don't
Do: See the pattern as shared.
Don't: Turn roles into identities.

Page Prompt
So you feel relief when they pull away—and panic when
they come back?

Reflection
Fearful–dismissive pairings can trigger safety and fear at
the same time.

Do / Don't
Do: Slow re-engagement intentionally.
Don't: Rush closeness to soothe anxiety.

Page Prompt
So reassurance is asked for—but hard to trust?

Reflection
Fearful–anxious dynamics amplify doubt because both systems are scanning for safety.

Do / Don't
Do: Regulate before seeking reassurance.
Don't: Demand certainty no one can promise.

Page Prompt
So you feel like you're constantly translating each other?

Reflection
Different attachment languages can make both partners feel
unseen.

Do / Don't
Do: Name differences without judgment.
Don't: Assume misunderstanding means incompatibility.

Page Prompt
So calm feels unfamiliar—and maybe even boring?

Reflection
Security can feel strange when chaos once felt normal.

Do / Don't
Do: Stay present long enough to recalibrate.
Don't: Create urgency to feel alive.

Page Prompt
So consistency makes you suspicious instead of relaxed?

Reflection
When unpredictability was familiar, steadiness can feel
unsafe at first.

Do / Don't
Do: Let stability unfold slowly.
Don't: Test it to see if it breaks.

Page Prompt
So you're growing—but the dynamic isn't changing?

Reflection
Healing one nervous system doesn't automatically heal the relationship.

Do / Don't
Do: Focus on your regulation.
Don't: Carry the relationship alone.

Page Prompt
So clarity shows up when you stop managing both sides?

Reflection
Clarity often arrives when you step out of the pattern.

Do / Don't
Do: Observe what changes when you respond differently.
Don't: Over-function to keep things going.

Page Prompt
So what if the problem isn't who you are—but how two attachment styles interact?

Reflection
Attachment dynamics take two nervous systems, not one flaw.

Do / Don't
Do: Release self-blame.
Don't: Personalize a pattern that requires mutual awareness.

PART VII

Page Prompt
So you're realizing you weren't confused—you were responding to something real?

Reflection
Clarity often arrives when you stop doubting your own experience.

Do / Don't
Do: Trust what your body has been telling you.
Don't: Rewrite your story to make others more comfortable.

Page Prompt
So you're noticing patterns instead of blaming yourself?

Reflection
Awareness replaces self-criticism with understanding.

Do / Don't
Do: Observe without judgment.
Don't: Turn insight into self-attack.

Page Prompt
So you're beginning to choose responses instead of
reactions?

Reflection
Regulation creates choice where survival once ruled.

Do / Don't
Do: Pause before engaging.
Don't: Expect perfection from yourself.

Page Prompt
So you're learning to stay with yourself during discomfort?

Reflection
Self-trust grows when you stop abandoning yourself.

Do / Don't
Do: Stay present with difficult feelings.
Don't: Leave yourself to keep peace.

Page Prompt
So you're realizing calm doesn't mean disconnection?

Reflection
Calm is often what safety feels like.

Do / Don't
Do: Let calm last longer than feels familiar.
Don't: Create urgency to feel alive.

Page Prompt
So you're allowing uncertainty without turning it into fear?

Reflection
Not knowing doesn't mean something is wrong.

Do / Don't
Do: Let questions exist gently.
Don't: Use uncertainty as proof you're failing.

Page Prompt
So you're trusting yourself more than the pattern?

Reflection
Self-trust grows quietly through consistent self-attunement.

Do / Don't
Do: Notice moments you chose yourself.
Don't: Minimize progress because it's subtle.

Page Prompt
So you're choosing clarity over confusion—even when it's
uncomfortable?

Reflection
Clarity is an act of self-respect.

Do / Don't
Do: Tell yourself the truth kindly.
Don't: Use honesty as punishment.

Page Prompt
So you're realizing wanting connection doesn't require self-abandonment?

Reflection
You don't have to disappear to belong.

Do / Don't
Do: Stay connected to yourself.
Don't: Trade self-respect for closeness.

Page Prompt
So you're learning that healing isn't dramatic—it's steady?

Reflection
Real change often feels quiet at first.

Do / Don't
Do: Trust small, consistent shifts.
Don't: Dismiss progress because it isn't intense.

Page Prompt
So you're realizing you can handle disappointment without
losing yourself?

Reflection
Resilience grows when self-abandonment stops.

Do / Don't
Do: Stay present through discomfort.
Don't: Run from feelings to avoid pain.

Page Prompt
So you're beginning to choose yourself—without closing
your heart?

Reflection
Self-alignment doesn't require emotional walls.

Do / Don't
Do: Choose what steadies you.
Don't: Protect yourself by shutting down.

Page Prompt
So what if nothing about you needs fixing?

Reflection
Understanding replaces self-judgment.

Do / Don't
Do: Carry this knowing forward.
Don't: Forget how far you've come.

Page Prompt
So if no one has told you this yet—let me be the one.

Reflection
You were never too much.
You were never broken.
And you were never asking for the wrong thing.

Do / Don't
Do: Remember this when old patterns resurface.
Don't: Doubt yourself into silence again.